A CURIOSITY for the CURIOUS

A Curiosity for the Curious

for the Curious

by HELEN REEDER CROSS

illustrated
by MARGOT TOMES

Coward, McCann & Geoghegan, Inc.
New York

Published simultaneously in Canada by
Longman Canada Limited, Toronto.
ISBN 0-698-20423-9
Designed by Cathy Altholz

Library of Congress Cataloguing in Publication Data
Cross, Helen Reeder.
    A Curiosity for the Curious.
    Summary: Relates how Hachaliah Bailey brought the
first elephant to the United States, toured the
East Coast with her, and thus began the first circus.
1. Bailey, Hachaliah—Juvenile fiction.
[1. Bailey, Hachaliah—Fiction.   2. Circus stories]
I. Tomes, Margot.   II. Title.
PZ7.C 26Cu   [Fic]   77-3400

Printed in the United States of America

The text type used in A CURIOSITY FOR THE CURIOUS is
14 point Plantin and the display characters are Rome, Coffee
Can, and Snell Roundhand photo lettering. The art work was
done in ink, pencil and gouache. Printed by offset, the book is
bound in paper over boards.

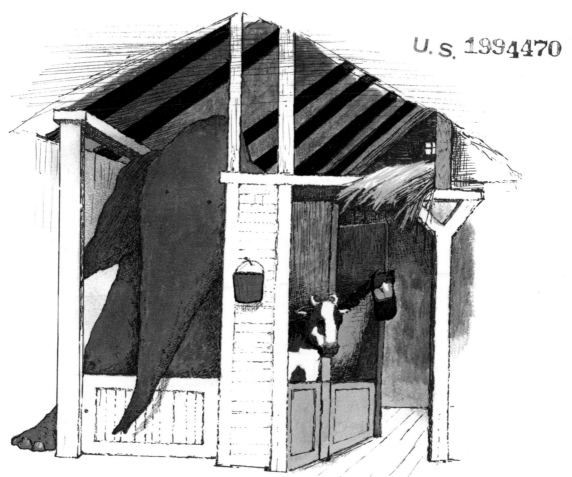

U. S. 1994470

for the littlest grandchild,
Jennifer,
to grow to

He had never seen one, of course, but Hachaliah Bailey loved elephants. If anybody except his brother Theodorus had told him about elephants, Hachaliah would have laughed at the tall tale. But Theodorus was captain of a clipper ship that sailed the Seven Seas, and Theodorus was not a man to stretch the truth.

In his last letter the sea captain had described the great beast called an "elyphunt." "Larger than any animal known to man," Theodorus had written. "Bigger than six horses rolled into one." (Hach found this hard to believe, in spite of his brother's reputation for telling the truth.) On the back of the paper Theodorus had drawn a picture of the strange creature.

Just thinking about its beady eyes and wispy tail amused Hach. So did imagining those enormous floppy ears. Most of all, Hachaliah Bailey admired that long nose called a trunk. According to Theodorus's letter, an elephant's trunk could pick up the tiniest acorn or the heaviest log from the ground. It could sniff a rose over a high fence. It could squirt water like a shower of April rain.

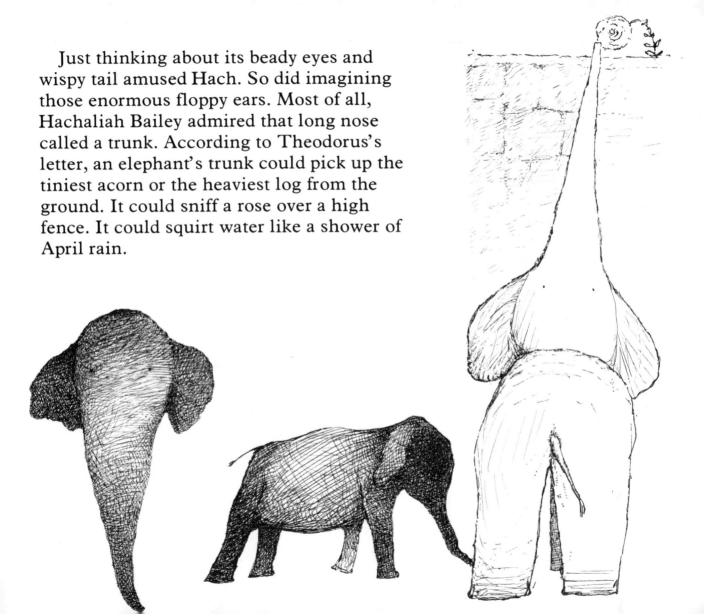

Suddenly Hachaliah had an idea. Why not ask his brother to bring one home from across the sea? In the early 1800's, in the village of Somers, New York, an elyphunt would be a curiosity for the curious. Hach felt sure a lot of people would give their eyeteeth to see one. Certainly he was one of those people.

Pretty soon Hachaliah had a plan. He would show this amazing creature called an elyphunt to all his neighbors. Furthermore, he would make them pay a pretty penny to see it. Who could tell? A real live elyphunt might even make his fortune. As far as Hachaliah Bailey knew, there had never been a pachyderm in all America. (This was true. There hadn't been.) He gave the matter considerable thought.

Hachaliah had always been a great thinker. ("Day-dreamer, I call it," his wife Azuba often said scornfully when his dreams burst like pricked bubbles. Like the time he had invented a cherry picker that didn't work. Or the time he had tried to train his

old hunting dog to stand on its hind legs as a trick.)

So while he did the spring plowing and sowing, Hach thought about elephants. While he hoed and chopped weeds, he thought about elephants. While he shucked corn and harvested apples, Hach was still thinking about elephants. When the first snow flew, he sat down to write a letter to Theodorus.

"If you could find me one of those elyphunt critters and sail it to New York," he wrote, "I'd be glad to pay you for your trouble. Not too high a price, you understand, but a reasonable sum."

There was a long wait before Theodorus's reply came—from England, of all places. The creature's name was "Old Bet." She had been born, no one knew how long ago, in the faraway land of India. Hachaliah's brother had found her offered for sale at an auction in London. There he had paid a handsome price for the great beast—all of $500.

Hachaliah swallowed hard when he read the price. But he would stick to his bargain, though he didn't mean to tell Azuba just yet. She would think he was daft. So would all the neighbors. Time enough to tell them when his elyphunt arrived at the dock in New York City.

So Hach calculated the time when Theodorus's clipper ship, the *Dolphin,* ought to land. When the time came he mustered the courage to tell Azuba about Old Bet. Although he said nothing about the price.

For once, Azuba was speechless. She gave her husband a startled stare, then continued her churning at a rate that would bring the butter in a hurry. Hach hustled himself out of the kitchen before Azuba could collect her wits and express her opinion about elyphunts. Though she had never seen one, Azuba would certainly have something to say on the subject.

Hach had all the money from last year's harvest in his pocket. It seemed this was the very time for a holiday in the city. With his old horse Dobbin pulling the wagon briskly, Hach set off in high spirits down the turnpike. He felt as free as dandelion fluff in a breeze. Even Dobbin pricked up her ears. The old horse seemed to step a mite livelier than usual all the way to the dock at Old Slip, in

New York's busy harbor.

It was a lovely summer morning when the *Dolphin* sailed into view. The great ship slipped into its moorings, its white sails drooping like the wings of a swan.

There was much commotion. Sailors shouted from the dock. Captain Theodorus Bailey was at the helm, barking orders to his men. He waved to his brother Hachaliah. There was much running and shouting. Bells rang. Whistles blew shrilly. Stevedores tied the ship's ropes to the dock.

At last the loading doors of the ship's hold opened. Hachaliah's eyes popped! For out stepped the largest land animal in all the world—an elephant. Its tiny eyes blinked in the bright sunshine. Its long rubbery trunk swung gently with every softly padding step, down the ship's gangplank to the dock.

The crowd on the wharf seemed to freeze. Shopkeepers stood spellbound in their doorways. Ladies with market baskets stared. Girls leaned dangerously from upstairs windows. Little children watched safely from behind their mothers' skirts. Gentlemen with high beaver hats gaped at the amazing spectacle. Boys shinnied up lampposts to see better, from a safe distance. The only sound on Old Slip wharf was the gentle lapping of small waves against the pier.

Hachaliah's thoughts raced wildly. By jingo! This elyphunt was as big as *two haystacks*, if not *three!* This critter would fill the barn back home in Somers. In fact, how would he get her home at all?

Come to think of it, what did elyphunts eat anyway? Hach began to feel nervous. What would Azuba say? She and the neighbors would think him addlepated for sure. This animal was much more than he had bargained for. But Hach was a man to stick to his bargains. He had hankered for an elyphunt, and nothing could stop him now.

His brother came ashore. The two men clapped each other soundly on the back in greeting. Then Hachaliah slowly counted out five new $100 bills and gave them to

Theodorus. One thing was certain. He didn't plan to tell Azuba how much he was paying for this elyphunt. Not yet anyway.

"She's yours," the captain said, "though by rights you ought to pay me more. Why, she ate three tons of hay while we were at sea and guzzled barrels more than her fair share of our water supply. Now tell me what in the name of common sense you want an elyphunt for?"

"Why, I figger she'll be a curiosity for the curious," Hachaliah replied with a swagger that he did not feel at the moment. "I reckon country folks will pay a pretty penny to see a fine elyphunt like this here Old Bet."

His brother looked doubtful.

"Well, I just hope you haven't wasted your good money," he said.

At last the moment had come. It was time for Hachaliah to make friends with an elephant. He turned and faced Old Bet.

Suddenly a man in the crowd found his voice.

"Look out!" he yelled to Hach. "That critter could eat a little man like you in two bites!"

A child in a red sunbonnet began to sob. Otherwise a body could have heard a pin drop on the wharf at Old Slip. Indeed, a shiver of fear crept up Hach's spine. Still, he remembered Theodorus's words in that letter. "This pachyderm may be a giant, but she won't hurt a flea."

So Hachaliah boldly stepped right up to the great creature. Though it gave him a turn, he tipped his head back and looked her straight in the eye. Man and elephant blinked at each other. Hachaliah took three hickory nuts from his pocket and offered them to Old Bet. Her trunk quivered slightly. Her ears flapped twice, like enormous gray fans. She looked at her new master but did not move. With his other hand Hach patted the elephant firmly on her trunk. People laughed nervously.

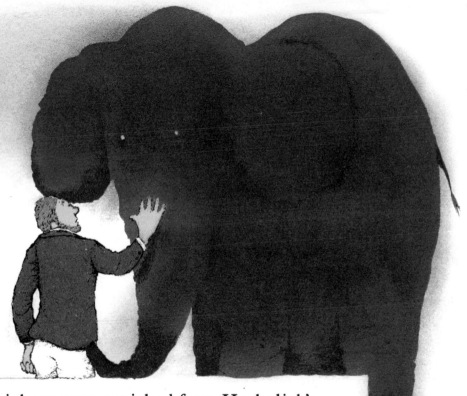

Suddenly the three hickory nuts vanished from Hachaliah's hand. Old Bet curved her trunk, put the nuts delicately into her mouth and began to chew. Before Hach could count to five, the tip of that trunk was tickling his back pocket. Old Bet liked those nuts and she wanted more!

The crowd seemed to breathe again. Everyone sighed happily. Old Bet was a gentle beast who would not eat Hachaliah in two bites or ten. Hach had made a friend.

"Now if somebody will just find me a rope," Hach said casually, "and a ladder too, I'll put a loop around Old Bet's neck. Then I reckon we'll be on our way up the Hudson River to home."

Immediately he had lots of help. Boys slid down those lampposts quick as a wink. Cautiously, they touched the elephant, then helped tie her. Somebody brought a bucket of water. Old Bet sucked it up so quickly with her trunk that men and boys had to pump more water from the well on the street corner. It took five buckets to satisfy the giant creature's thirst.

When Hach sat high on the wagon seat, Old Bet could have tickled him with her trunk, if she had a mind to.

"Giddyap!" he said to Dobbin. Off went horse, wagon, and Hachaliah. Old Bet padded softly behind.

What a sight it was! A policeman on the corner of Broad Street and Bowery Road forgot to blow his whistle. Horses refused to pull a crowded trolley car past the strange beast and caused a traffic jam. People stared and screamed and whistled—some in fright, all in wonder. What a curiosity! A dozen boys trailed behind Old Bet. Some turned cartwheels. All were glad to be seen as part of the little procession.

As for Hachaliah, he was proud as a peacock spreading his tail.

"Glory be!" he said to himself. "All these people! Who says folks don't hanker to see an elyphunt? But they're getting a free look at Bet today. We'll put a quick stop to this, or I'll never see that $500 again."

So he took his elephant to the Hudson River docks, where he hired a sloop. It would take him, his horse and wagon and Old Bet upriver.

It was a three-day sail to Peekskill, where the sloop landed late at
night. There was no moon. Hachaliah unloaded Bet by lantern
light. She plodded softly behind the wagon the rest of the way
home to the village of Somers.

At last they came to Hachaliah's farm. Hach led Old Bet to the
barn. She could hardly squeeze through the doors cut the size of a
hay wagon. There was precious little room left in that barn when
Old Bet, Dobbin, and Azuba's cow were all inside. But the animals
didn't seem to mind.

Next morning Azuba took a safe look through a knothole in the barn door.

Her eyes popped. "Mercy sakes!" she gasped. "Hachaliah Bailey, have you taken leave of your senses? What in the name of heaven do you call that critter?"

"It's an elyphunt," Hach told her. He stepped inside the barn and patted Old Bet's trunk proudly.

"Why, it scares the wits out of me just to look at that beast through a knothole!" Azuba said. "I'll never dare set foot in our own barn again. I don't hanker to be trampled flat as a flounder by those great feet. And I don't want that terrible nose to touch me—ever! What in tarnation do you plan to do with an elyphunt anyway? Nobody but you has ever heard tell of such a curiosity."

"That's just it, Azuba," Hachaliah replied. "I figger there's a lot of folks just like me. They may not be in their right minds either. But I bet my bottom dollar they'll be willing

to pay as much as a quarter of a dollar each to see a live elyphunt from the other side of the world. Old Bet is a curiosity for the curious."

Hachaliah was right as rain. News of Old Bet spread like the measles. Soon everybody in Somers had paid a visit to Hachaliah's barn. The village supervisor came. So did the teacher from the little red schoolhouse. The preacher and the storekeeper came. So did farm families from miles around.

Even the stingiest grownups thought it "educational" to pay all of 25 cents to see an elyphunt from faraway India. Children paid only a shilling each. Some had to pick apples all day to earn that shilling. Others weeded their mothers' strawberry patches.

He printed posters which he sent ahead to
be stuck on fences. These said:

A CURIOSITY FOR THE CURIOUS!
HOLD YER HOSSES!
AN ELYPHUNT IS COMING TO TOWN!
SHE GOES BY THE NAME OF "OLD BET."
SHE WAS BORN IN THE LAND OF INDIA.
NOW SHE BELONGS TO HACHALIAH BAILEY
OF SOMERS, NEW YORK.
THIS REAL LIVE PACHYDERM
IS AS BIG AS TWO HAYSTACKS.
SEE HER IN TULLEY'S TAVERN YARD
FROM SUNUP TO SUNDOWN
ON JULY 1

ADMISSION: A QUARTER OF A DOLLAR
—CHILDREN: ONE SHILLING

Hachaliah soon found that it takes more than hickory nuts to feed an elephant (though hickory nuts were still her favorite treat, snitched from Hach's back pocket when he wasn't looking). Instead of paying to see her, dozens of boys were hired to carry water for Bet. Farmers bartered bales of hay, bushels of potatoes, and baskets of cabbages for her to eat, instead of parting with a quarter of a dollar.

At last everyone in Somers had had a good look—some of them three or four looks. It was time to take Old Bet to a new town. As if Bet herself were not enough to attract attention, Hachaliah painted the wagon bright red.

From town to town they went all summer long, moving only at night so no one could see Old Bet for free. They traveled many miles of turnpikes in both bright sun and pouring rain. When those country roads were deep with mud, Old Bet pushed or pulled the wagon from the mire as easily as if it were a feather. Mostly she padded contentedly behind, a rope tied loosely around her neck.

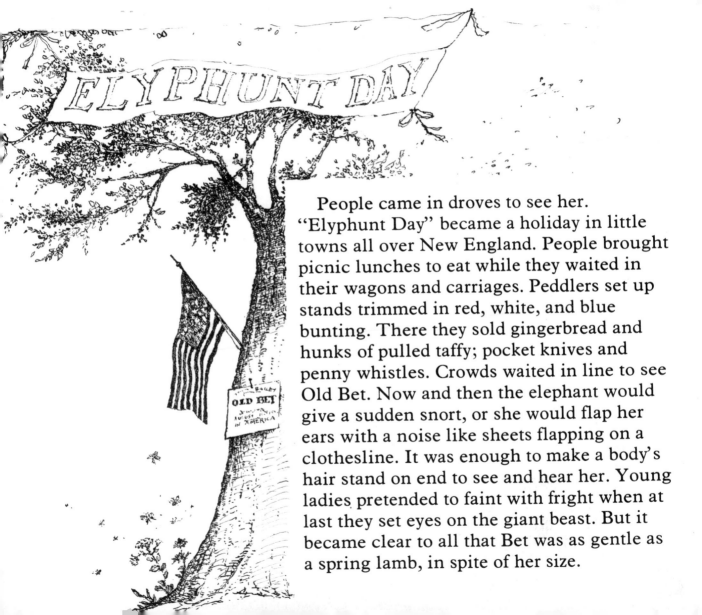

ELYPHUNT DAY

OLD BET

People came in droves to see her. "Elyphunt Day" became a holiday in little towns all over New England. People brought picnic lunches to eat while they waited in their wagons and carriages. Peddlers set up stands trimmed in red, white, and blue bunting. There they sold gingerbread and hunks of pulled taffy; pocket knives and penny whistles. Crowds waited in line to see Old Bet. Now and then the elephant would give a sudden snort, or she would flap her ears with a noise like sheets flapping on a clothesline. It was enough to make a body's hair stand on end to see and hear her. Young ladies pretended to faint with fright when at last they set eyes on the giant beast. But it became clear to all that Bet was as gentle as a spring lamb, in spite of her size.

Because her husband was not there to mend a hole in the barnyard fence, Azuba lost three of her best laying hens. She had planned to buy a new bonnet with egg money from those hens. To her way of thinking, Hach had never had one grain of sense about money. Azuba had no notion how much it was costing to feed that critter. So one day she put her foot down.

"Those sweet cherries on my grandmother's tree are ripe," she told Hach. "There never was such a lovely crop. I don't hanker after climbing that tree myself to pick those cherries. And I haven't forgotten that silly contraption you invented once for cherry-picking. So this time if you want cherry pie," she said sharply, "you'd better stay home long enough to pick them yourself. Instead of traipsing all over Kingdom Come with that elyphunt of yours."

Hachaliah didn't argue, for a clever idea had popped into his head. It had occurred to Hach that the best possible cherry-picker was a member of the Bailey family.

After breakfast he quietly led Old Bet into the orchard. By this time he and the elephant understood each other almost without words. Hach showed her the cherries and the bushel basket set under the tree.

To encourage her, Hach picked a handful of the bright red fruit for her to taste. It was a terrible mistake! In a trice Old Bet began stripping the tree of its dark sweet cherries. However, she ignored the basket. She ignored Hach's pleas too, even when he pulled her wispy tail *hard*—something she did not usually like at all. In half an hour the tree was completely bare. Old Bet had eaten every cherry.

Hachaliah was crestfallen. He was worried too. What would Azuba do? He soon found out. She was furious, but she didn't speak a word. There was no cherry pie for supper. In fact, Azuba offered her husband no dessert at all.

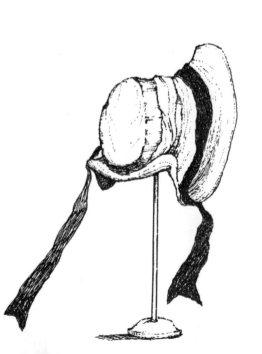

All that night, instead of sleeping, Azuba got madder and madder. Next morning at breakfast she had found her tongue.

"Folks are saying I married a fool," she told Hach sharply. "They may be right. Who but a fool would care more about an elyphunt than about his farm or his wife? Why, I haven't had a new Sunday bonnet for five years. And I've been hankering for a rocking chair. But instead of buying nice things for me, you spend a fortune on food for that critter!"

Hach gulped and knew the time had come to tell Azuba everything. He told her the whole story about the $500 he had paid for Old Bet. And about how that debt had been cleared long ago.

"In fact," he told her proudly, "you're on your way to being a mighty rich woman, thanks to that elyphunt."

Before he and Old Bet set off down the turnpike that day, Azuba had money in her apron pocket—enough for a bonnet and a rocking chair and for a hired man to do chores on the farm.

As for Hach, now that Azuba knew the whole story, he traveled with a light heart. It felt good to ride high and free on the red wagon, leading his elyphunt to a new village.

There seemed no end to the country folk who would welcome him and his Old Bet. But as time went on, Hach found he needed a bit of help. So in each town he hired two likely boys. One played a drum up and down the streets and sold tickets. The other gave away handbills which announced Old Bet's arrival in large black letters:

HERE SHE COMES!
OLD BET,
THE FIRST PACHYDERM IN
ALL AMERICA!
HACHALIAH BAILEY
DECLARES AUGUST 6 TO BE
ELYPHUNT DAY IN THIS TOWN.
COME TO THE OLD SALT TAVERN YARD
FROM SUNUP TO SUNDOWN
ADMISSION: A QUARTER OF A DOLLAR
—CHILDREN: ONE SHILLING

One of these boys was named Phineas Taylor Barnum. Hach hired him in the beginning of summer and, from the first, they hit it off. For one thing, young Phineas had a way with Old Bet. The elephant would let the lad scrub her down with a stiff broom after her daily shower in the nearest brook.

Phineas and Bet became fast friends after one famous night when Bet woke the whole village of Somers with wild trumpeting. The earth seemed to shake with her thunder. Azuba quaked in her bed with a blanket pulled over her head.

Hach and Phineas ran to the barn and found Bet whimpering in a corner, all atremble. Tears streamed from her tiny eyes at the sight of three mice who were busy nibbling her oats. Phineas caught the mice by tossing his cap over them. Then he and Hachaliah had a good laugh. To think that an elephant would be afraid of a mouse! Still, it made sense when they thought about it. What elephant would risk having a mouse climb into her sensitive trunk by mistake? The very thought was enough to terrify the bravest pachyderm.

After this episode Phineas traveled for the rest of that summer with Hach and Old Bet. She trusted him enough to let the boy do what only Hach had done before. Phineas was allowed to thrust his hand into the elephant's mouth in greeting every morning. It was a sign of trust, like a slap on the shoulder between friends.

Together Hach and Phineas began to teach Old Bet a few tricks. She was bright as a silver dollar. They taught her to balance her four feet on a wooden washtub, turned upside down. They taught her to wave the American flag at the end of her trunk to the whistled tune of "Yankee Doodle." She learned to stack a tavern keeper's winter firewood in half an hour. She learned to pick up Hachaliah or Phineas with her trunk and set them gently on her broad back for a ride. Best of all, she learned to dance a few clumsy steps to the lively music of Phineas T. Barnum's fife. Hachaliah taught her to do this by tapping her knees one at a time lightly with a stick.

In all their born days, people had never dreamed of seeing a giant pachyderm perform such tricks. Old Bet was happy to do them, for, after every trick well done, her master gave her a piece of licorice candy. Licorice was Old Bet's favorite flavor. She liked candy even better than hickory nuts.

But sometimes Bet did tricks of her own. Hach was sure she had her own secret sense of humor. One day she grabbed a bag of popcorn from a boy and ate every kernel. Once Bet snatched a wig from the head of a fat man. She waved it high in the air, just out of reach. People laughed (all except the man himself), for the wig looked like a yellow bird's nest. Old Bet's eyes seemed to twinkle as she set the wig back on the angry man's bald head. Another time she plucked a lace handkerchief from a lady's pocket.

Bet often picked a pink rose over the top of a high board fence, for pink was her favorite color. She was especially partial to little girls in pink dresses. Hach had to keep a sharp eye out, for if Bet saw such a child, she lifted her high in the air with her trunk before a body could say "Skeedaddle!" This habit worried some mothers.

Her tricks drove Hachaliah wild. Because of them he never dared turn his back when they were doing a show. Once or twice the elephant scared the wits out of people by trumpeting loudly for no reason at all. When Bet trumpeted, the sound was like a foghorn. And she liked nothing quite so much as tossing hay on children who dared to pull her tail. Unless it was spraying water on small boys wearing their Sunday clothes. It kept Hach on his toes to see that Bet behaved.

Still, one time Bet's love of spraying water came in handy. They were in a small Vermont town. In the middle of the night someone yelled, "FIRE!" Hachaliah jumped out of bed in his nightshirt. A house was burning! Flames lighted the sky. Smoke billowed from the roof. Quickly, men of the town formed a bucket brigade. From hand to hand they passed pails of water from Peter's Pond to the fire. But ugly flames flashed higher and higher.

Hachaliah had an idea. He ran to Bet's barn. She was already wide awake and booming like thunder. Her ears flapped wildly. No doubt she felt the excitement in the air and smelled the fire. Like all animals, she feared fire.

Hach untied her and rushed Bet into the street. People scattered out of her way. Hach led Bet straight to Peter's Pond, where she seemed to know by instinct exactly what to do.

Quick as summer lightning she filled her trunk with water, then ran to squirt it on the burning house. In spite of her great size, she

was faster than the men with the pails. Back and forth she padded. Hachaliah encouraged her at every clumsy step. Bet even seemed to enjoy the wild excitement of this night. Between squirts she squealed and flapped her ears in glee. No wonder she was happy. For once, Hach was not telling her to stop spraying water. In fact, people were shouting, "More! More! Out of the way! Let Bet do it!"

Finally the fire died down. Every spark flickered out. "Hooray! Hooray for Bet!" the villagers cheered. "She puts the fire brigade in the shade!" Hachaliah was as proud of his elephant as if she were his own clever child.

Next day the village gave Old Bet a peck of peanuts. Boys and girls made a sunflower chain to hang on her neck. They crowned Bet, "Her Highness, Queen Of Elyphunts."

"Let us buy Old Bet from you," the village people begged Hachaliah. "We'll pay whatever you ask for your elyphunt. We promise to feed her well. She'll be our town pet and put out all our fires besides."

"Why, I wouldn't sell the critter for a fortune," Hachaliah said. No wonder. For Old Bet had made him a very rich man by this time. More than that, she was the best animal friend a body ever had.

Even Azuba was becoming a mite proud of Old Bet. To tell the truth, she had become a mite proud of her husband also, perhaps because he *was* a little daft. What other man in all the land would have dreamed of buying an elyphunt from the other side of the world? What other man would dare ride high on the critter's back, as cool as a cucumber? And what other man could have become rich from such a crazy scheme?

So Azuba had a surprise waiting for Hachaliah, next time he came home. It was a kind of peace offering. It was really a surprise for Bet. Azuba had made a red velvet saddlecloth to fold over the elephant's broad back. Old Bet looked as proud of her present as a child with a new jacket. Hachaliah was delighted. Azuba's gift gave him a new notion. He had a harness made for the elephant's neck and a headdress with elegant tassels. These were all of red velvet, trimmed with gold braid.

"Why don't you take the first ride on the velvet trappings?" Hach asked Azuba hopefully. "Bet will lift you like a feather up to her back. You'll feel like a pretty bird perched on the limb of a giant tree. She'll even hold a sunshade over your head."

"Thank you, no," Azuba replied politely but firmly. She turned pale at such an idea. "I'm not likely to trust any wild critter that much. Not from now 'til Kingdom Come. But I reckon I might offer her a little treat for once."

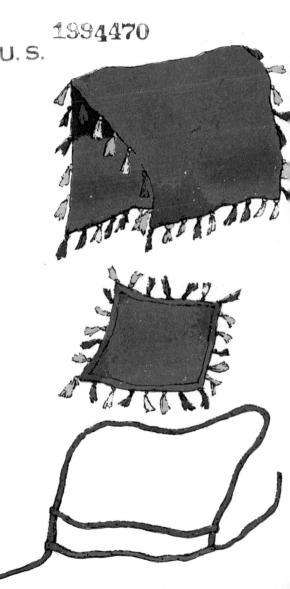

Then Azuba held out her hand for the very first time to the great creature of which she had been so fearful. That hand trembled only a little. Old Bet delicately took the piece of licorice candy from it with the tip of her trunk. It had taken a month of Sundays, but at last Azuba and Old Bet seemed to be friends. Hach preened his feathers. It seemed a real victory.

On the Fourth of July Old Bet wore her red-velvet finery for the first time for all to see. With her old friend, Phineas T. Barnum, on her back, she marched grandly down the village street of Somers. People had gathered on the green to wave flags and admire their very own elyphunt. Hachaliah wore a spanking new swallow-tailed coat and a beaver hat. Azuba wore a fine leghorn bonnet with a green ribbon. She carried a silk sunshade to match. It was a proud moment.

"I knew you'd come to like Old Bet," Hach told his wife. "You always were a right smart woman." He squeezed Azuba's elbow lovingly. "I'm a lucky feller, with the spunkiest wife and the finest elyphunt in the world." Then he peeped anxiously under the brim of her bonnet to be sure Azuba was in a good mood.

"Now it's time, I reckon, to tell you about another little notion I've dreamed up lately."

Azuba looked startled, but said nothing.

Hach swallowed hard, then continued.

"A feller told me t'other day about some new critters he saw in New York. Fresh-come they were from Africa. A 'giraffe' and a passel of 'monkeys,' he called them. I've half a mind to buy the lot to travel with Old Bet and me next spring. What a sight we'd be for the country folks!" Hach's eyes shone with excitement. Then he stopped, for Azuba was staring at him strangely. Her cheeks were pink; her eyes flashed.

"Hachaliah Bailey!" she gasped. "Are you plumb crazy? Here I've just begun to tolerate an elyphunt. I don't hanker for a Noah's Ark in our barn!"

"Now, now, Azuba," Hach said gently. His eyes still had that dreamy, faraway look that Azuba knew all too well. "Just think of the tricks I could teach those monkeys. Folks say they're right smart, almost as smart as Bet. Of course that can't be true. There's no animal as pert as an elyphunt, especially Old Bet. But I kind of hanker to see for myself."

Hach waved as Phineas rode by on Bet's back, then continued dreaming aloud. "Think of it, Azuba! What a sight we'd be: Bet with her red velvet trappings, carrying a little dressed-up monkey on her back. And a spotted giraffe behind, bowing his long neck with every step at *Her Highness, Queen Of Elyphunts*. What a sight for sore eyes that would be!"

But Azuba had made up her mind at last. She looked her husband straight in the eye and said firmly, "Enough is enough! It isn't Old Bet who's a curiosity for the curious, Hachaliah. It's you!"

And right in front of all the good folk of Somers, New York, Azuba hit her husband soundly on the head with her new green sunshade.

AUTHOR'S NOTE:

There was indeed a man named Hachaliah Bailey who lived in the village of Somers, New York, in the early 1800's. He was the proud owner of an elephant named "Old Bet." Many people believe her to have been the first pachyderm in all America. Hachaliah paraded her up and down the land as this story tells and became a rich man because of Old Bet.

Hach later added a few other animals to his traveling show, as well. To this day Hachaliah Bailey is called the "Father of the American Circus." This title would have surprised Hach, for "Circus" is a word he probably never heard in all his life. In his day such a show was called, "An Educational Exhibit."

His young helper, Phineas T. Barnum, grew up to be one of the owners of the *Barnum and Bailey Circus.* For many years it has been called, "The Greatest Show on Earth." Phineas no doubt learned much about the art of ballyhoo from his first boss, Hachaliah. He also learned that people will cheerfully pay their hard-earned money for the privilege of seeing strange and marvellous sights, like Old Bet. Later, other wonders were added (like trained seals and trapeze artists, midgets and sword swallowers). How Hachaliah's eyes would have popped at seeing them!

After many years of traveling up and down the countryside, Old Bet died in Maine. Later Hach built a hotel where the turnpikes crossed in Somers. He named this the "Elephant Hotel," in memory of Old Bet, whom he had loved in a special way. The hotel is still there today. It is now the Town Hall of Somers.

In front there is a small grass plot, on which Hachaliah set a tall post. On its tip he placed a wooden elephant, painted gold. Today the gilt has weathered away but if you look closely, you can see it is a model of Old Bet herself.

There are a circus museum and a library in the Elephant Hotel. If you go there you will see pictures of the real Old Bet. Her velvet trappings, with their golden tassels now tarnished, lie in a glass case for all to see. There are posters too from long-ago fences. One old handbill called Bet, "The greatest natural curiosity ever presented to the curious."

Even now, nearly every year an elephant from one of America's great modern circuses is walked all the way from New York City to Somers. There, with much ballyhoo of cameras and newspapermen, this elephant lays a wreath of flowers at the foot of Old Bet's monument.